A MESSAGE TO PARENTS

It is of vital importance for parents to read good books to young children in order to aid the child's psychological and intellectual development. At the same time as stimulating the child's imagination and awareness of his environment, it creates a positive relationship between parent and child. The child will gradually increase his basic vocabulary and will soon be able to read books alone.

Brown Watson has published this series of books with these aims in mind. By collecting this inexpensive library, parent and child are provided with hours of pleasurable and profitable reading.

Santa's
Little Helper

Text by Maureen Spurgeon

Brown Watson

ENGLAND

It was always cold where Peter lived – almost as cold as the land where Santa Claus came from. And with all the ice and snow and the green fir trees reaching up to the sky, everywhere always looked Christmassy, too – especially when Peter and his dad came back from town on the sledge!

The sledge was always loaded up
when Christmas was coming. Not
with toys and presents, but with
food, clothes and everything else
Peter's family needed. A team of
dogs pulled it across the snow.

Peter loved all the dogs and
helped to look after each one.
His favourite was Marcus, the
leader. "Daddy," Peter said one
day, "why does Santa Claus have
reindeer to pull his sleigh?"

"I suppose, because he's always
had reindeer," smiled Daddy.
"I just happen to like dogs best."
"So do I!" said Peter. "Marcus
could pull the sleigh across the
sky without any trouble."

Peter went indoors to write his Christmas letter. What he wanted more than anything else was a guitar. "My Daddy could teach me how to play it," he wrote, "and everyone would enjoy the music."

Peter finished by writing about his clever dog, Marcus. But he was wondering if Santa Claus really could bring the guitar he wanted so badly. He had only ever seen a picture of one, in a book.

An icy blast of wind lifted Peter's letter up and up into the dark, wintry sky, until it was like a big snowflake, whirling round and round. Then, at last, it floated down on a cloud.

At least, it looked like a cloud to anyone who might have been watching. But really, it was a heap of letters. "We'll never get all these sorted out!" someone cried. "It's Christmas Eve, soon!"

"We'll manage!" came a jolly-sounding voice, and a chubby hand in a red sleeve picked up Peter's letter. "How many times have I said that Christmas comes but once a year?"

But even Santa Claus had to admit that he and his workshops did seem to be extra busy! There was so much to do! Toys to be sorted out, presents wrapped and loaded on to his sleigh . . . .

"Mind out, Prancer!" puffed Santa Claus, helping to drag a big sack of toys across the snow. "Ooh, I'll be glad to get this lot on the sleigh. Then I think we'll have a nice cup of tea . . . ."

Poor Santa! His hands were so cold that the edge of the sack slipped from his fingers.
Teddy Bears, footballs, cars, games . . . . out they all tumbled, rolling around on the snow!

Poor Prancer! He stepped back
on a big, toy engine – and down
he went, too!
"Prancer!" cried Santa Claus in
alarm. "Prancer, are you all
right?"

"No Christmas Eve duties for you, boy!" said Santa Claus seeing his hurt leg. Prancer was very upset. And Santa knew the other reindeer could not pull the heavy sleigh without him . . . .

All was quiet that Christmas Eve. Everyone had been working hard. Now all that could be heard was the rustle of coal as it shifted on the fire and the whisper of snow against the window.

Peter was fast asleep, dreaming of everyone singing and dancing to his guitar, just as he had told Santa Claus. He did not hear a low whistle outside in the snow. But someone else did . . . .

"Here, Marcus, old boy!" called Santa Claus softly. Marcus soon appeared. "Peter told me all about you. Would you like to help pull my sleigh?" Marcus wagged his tail without stopping.

Santa Claus put on the jangly harness, just like Peter fastened the straps when Marcus pulled the sledge. But, as soon as he stepped out with the reindeer – can you guess what happened?

The sleigh lifted up into the sky, stars twinkling all around! "Get some speed up!" cried Santa Claus, shaking the reins with a merry, jingling sound. "Lots to do before Christmas morning!"

And so there was. Hundreds o
chimney stacks, thousands o
roofs, across towns, big cities
and villages! Santa Claus and his
sleigh visited them all. Marcus
had never seen such sights!

Dawn was just beginning to break as Santa Claus steered the sleigh back to Peter's home. "Thanks for your help, Marcus!" he said, giving him a pat. "We'd never have managed without you!"

Peter got up early next morning
"Do you know," he said sleepily, "
had a lovely dream last night. It
was all about Marcus going with
Santa Claus, helping the reindeer
to pull his sleigh!"

"You were asking me if I thought Marcus could do the job," Daddy smiled. "So maybe you went to bed wondering about it. Anyway, come and see what Santa Claus has left you."

There were sweets, toys – and a
big parcel with a label tied on it
"DEAR PETER," it read, "HERE IS A
SPECIAL PRESENT FOR TELLING
ME ABOUT YOUR DOG, MAR-
CUS. HE WAS A GREAT HELP TO
ME AND MY REINDEER!"
Peter did not know which he